Curti

SIMON AND SCHUSTER
BOOKS FOR YOUNG READERS
Simon & Schuster Building, Rockefeller Center
1230 Avenue of the Americas, New York, New York 10020

Originally published in Great Britain by Faber and Faber Limited.
First U.S. edition 1990
SIMON AND SCHUSTER BOOKS FOR YOUNG READERS
is a trademark of Simon & Schuster Inc.
Manufactured in Belgium

10 9 8 7 6 5 4 3 2 1

Library of Congress Cataloging-in-Publication Data
Riddell, Chris.   The bear dance / written and illustrated by Chris
Riddell.   Summary: When Jack Frost brings gray winter to a forest where
it is always summer, a young girl brings sunlight back by engaging
Mr. Frost in a vigorous Bear Dance.   [1. Jack Frost—Fiction.
2. Dancing—Fiction. 3. Bears—Fiction.] I. Title.
PZ7.R41618Bd 1990   90-9475
[E]—dc20   CIP   AC
ISBN 0-671-70974-7

BOMC offers recordings and compact discs, cassettes
and records. For information and catalog write to
BOMR, Camp Hill, PA 17012.

CURTI

The Bear Dance

WRITTEN AND ILLUSTRATED BY

CHRIS RIDDELL

Simon and Schuster Books for Young Readers

Published by Simon & Schuster Inc.
New York • London • Toronto • Sydney • Tokyo • Singapore

Katya lived in the middle of a great forest where it was always summer. Her best friend was a big, bumbly bear called Brown.

After a hard day spent picking flowers, climbing trees and paddling in the river, Katya and Brown would have supper on the old tree stump in the middle of the forest clearing. After they had eaten and cleared away the plates, Brown would bow very low and say in his grumbly, bumbly voice, "Would you care for the next dance?" And Katya always replied, "Yes, please!"

Then together they danced the Charleston,
the Fox trot, the Waltz . . .

the Cancan, and an elegant tap dance on the table.

But they always saved the best dance till last. In the middle of the forest clearing, with only the far-off hoot of an owl to disturb the peace, they would throw themselves into the stomping, shouting, growling, thumping, stamping, jumping-in-the-air Bear Dance!

And when they fell down exhausted in a heap, Brown would look at the moon and say, "Goodness! Is that the time?" And he would shuffle into his cave, and Katya would climb the Sleeping Tree and sleep there without waking until daylight.

One morning, Katya woke with a shiver. The sky was gray with clouds and the sun was nowhere to be seen. A couple of snowflakes drifted down. "I must go and tell Brown," Katya thought. "This has never happened in my forest before."

"Brown!" called Katya. "Brown, wake up! The sky is gray and the ground is turning white!" But the only answer from inside Brown's cave was the sound of his deep, grumbly, bumbly snoring. "I'll get to the bottom of this," Katya said to herself, and she set off for the forest clearing.

By the time Katya reached the clearing, the forest was white and her fingers and toes were numb with cold. She stood on the old tree stump and looked about her. "Oh, what has happened to my forest?" she cried. "It's my forest now," an icy voice replied. And there in the clearing stood a strange figure in a great white cloak, with an icicle on the end of his nose. "This is Jack Frost's forest now!"

Katya glared. She was cold and tired. "Sleep, Katya, sleep in the lovely soft snow," wheedled Jack Frost in his crackly, frosty voice. But Katya knew that was a bad idea. So she stamped her feet and blew on her fingers and said, "If you want me to go to sleep, Mister Snowy Frosty Jack with the icicle nose, you'll have to dance with me first!" Then she bowed low and said, "Would you care for the next dance?" "I'll dance with you," said Jack Frost, "but you won't get your forest back!"

Together they danced the Charleston, the Fox trot, the Waltz, the Cancan, and an elegant tap dance on the table. Then, gathering all her strength, Katya shouted, "And now we'll dance the Bear Dance!"

Round and round the clearing they went,
faster and faster, dancing the stomping,
shouting, growling, thumping, stamping,
jumping-in-the-air Bear Dance!

Finally, Katya could dance no more and collapsed in a
heap on the green forest floor. Jack Frost was nowhere to
be seen . . .

"What's for breakfast?" said Brown in his bumbly,
grumbly voice, as he shuffled into the forest clearing.
    But there was no reply. Katya lay
happily asleep in the warm sunlight.